Saggy Baggy Elephant
No Place for Me

By Gina Ingoglia
Illustrated by Richard Walz

A GOLDEN BOOK • NEW YORK
Western Publishing Company, Inc., Racine, Wisconsin 53404

Copyright © 1989 Western Publishing Company, Inc. All rights reserved. Printed in the U.S.A. No part of this book may be reproduced or copied in any form without written permission from the publisher. GOLDEN®, GOLDEN & DESIGN®, A GOLDEN BOOK®, A LITTLE GOLDEN BOOK®, and LITTLE GOLDEN BOOK LAND & associated character names and likenesses are trademarks of Western Publishing Company, Inc. Library of Congress Catalog Card Number: 88-50938 ISBN: 0-307-00043-5 A B C D E F G H I J K L M

There is a magical place called Little Golden Book Land, filled with wonderful things to see and do. Every day is a special day, just waiting to be discovered.

Saggy Baggy Elephant woke up late. He
hurried to the big playing field in Homeway
Hollow. Everybody was there, practicing for
Carnival Day. Saggy Baggy Elephant didn't
know what he was going to do in the carnival, but
he was sure it would be fun!

"Hi, Saggy," said five little clowns. It was Poky Little Puppy and his brothers and sisters.

Saggy Baggy Elephant laughed. "You look great!" he said.

"Would you like to join us?" asked Poky Little Puppy.

"I'm afraid he can't," said one of Poky's
brothers. "We don't have enough makeup to
cover us and all of Saggy's wrinkles."

"Or his trunk," added Poky's sister.

"That's all right," said Saggy Baggy Elephant.
"I'll find something else to do."

Saggy Baggy Elephant heard a loud roar. His friend Tawny Scrawny Lion was practicing his act in front of a group of rabbits.

"Hi, Saggy," said Tawny Scrawny Lion. "Why don't you join me with your trumpeting?"

The two friends roared and trumpeted together. The ground shook and the tall trees swayed with the noise.

"Too loud! Too loud!" shouted all the rabbits, hopping up and down and holding their ears.

"Sorry," said Tawny Scrawny Lion. "I guess this is a one-man act."

"Thanks anyway," said Saggy Baggy Elephant. "I'll look around some more."

"Saggy, watch this," called Baby Brown Bear. He was balancing upside down on a big rubber ball.

"That's really something," said Saggy Baggy Elephant. "I wish I could do that."

Baby Brown Bear scrambled to the ground. "Why don't you try it?" he suggested.

Saggy Baggy Elephant tried to climb up on the ball, but he flipped over and landed with his feet in the air.

"I bent my trunk a little," he said, straightening it out. "I'd better look for another act."

"Whee, whee, look at me!" sang a tiny voice. It was Shy Little Kitten. She was jumping up and down on a trampoline.

"I'm surprised to see you performing in the carnival," said Saggy Baggy Elephant. "You are usually so shy."

The little kitten finished a triple backflip and
landed on her four paws.

"I'm not doing this alone," she said. "It's a
family act. Cats always land on their feet, you
know. Would you like to give it a try?"

Saggy Baggy Elephant's trunk still hurt a little.

"I've done enough flipping for one day,"
he said.

Saggy Baggy Elephant was getting worried. He was running out of things to try. He decided to stop and think.

"I'm strong and I can carry things with my trunk," he said to himself. "Those are things I can do well."

In the distance he could hear Tootle the steam engine. He was blowing his whistle somewhere in Little Golden Book Land.

"That's it!" Saggy Baggy Elephant cried. "I'll help Tootle carry supplies and passengers to the carnival."

He ran alongside the train tracks, looking for his friend.

Tootle was down at the harbor with Scuffy the tugboat and Katy Caboose.

"Do you need help?" asked Saggy Baggy Elephant, running up to them.

"We're all finished," said Tootle. "I just dropped off the last load for the carnival. Now I'm going there myself. But, first, would you like to race?"

"No, thanks," said Saggy Baggy Elephant in a sad little voice. "I think I'll go home for a while."

Saggy Baggy Elephant slowly headed back
toward the Jolly Jungle.

"There's nothing for me to do at the carnival,"
he said with a sigh.

The little elephant stopped to nibble on some tall grass. Then he ate a few nice-looking flowers. He could hear a band playing at the carnival, and he tried not to listen. Saggy Baggy Elephant was sure the music would make him sad, because it would remind him that he wasn't a part of the carnival.

But, instead, the music sounded nice.

"It makes me feel like dancing," he said. "I haven't done that for a long time. Maybe it will cheer me up."

Saggy Baggy Elephant began to dance. He thumped his big feet on the ground—one-two-three-kick! One-two-three-kick!

"That's pretty good," said a voice. It was one of the older elephants from his herd.

"Really?" asked Saggy Baggy Elephant. "Do you think it's too thumpy and bumpy?"

"It's thumpy and bumpy, all right, but it's nice, and different, too," answered the older elephant. "Why don't you dance in the carnival?"

"I'd like that," said Saggy Baggy Elephant.

ants went back to the carnival.
ilies," shouted the older
ound. I'd like to present the
Saggy Baggy Elephant."
t danced and thumped,
nd cheered.

Tawny Scrawny Lion ran up to him.
"I didn't know you could dance," he said.
"Isn't it hard?" asked Shy Little Kitten.
"It's fun," said Saggy Baggy Elephant. "I'll teach you. All together, everybody! One-two-three-kick! One-two-three-kick!"